Scarlett

BY RISA BECKETT ILLUSTRATED BY DARWIN MARFIL

A POST HILL PRESS BOOK

ISBN: 978-1-64293-002-3

Cover art and interior illustrations by Darwin Marfil
Interior typography and layout by Greg Johnson, Textbook Perfect

Sources
https://kids.nationalgeographic.com
https://www.nationalgeographic.com
https://www.arkive.org
https://www.britannica.com
http://animals.sandiegozoo.org/animals/capybara
http://animals.sandiegozoo.org/animals/jaguar
https://www.nationalgeographic.com/animals/mammals/o/ocelot
https://www.nationalgeographic.com/animals/mammals/g/golden-lion-tamarin
https://www.nationalgeographic.com/search/?q=giant+anteater

PRESS

Post Hill Press
New York · Nashville
posthillpress.com

Published in the United States of America
Printed in China

For my beautiful daughter, Nicole, whose
passion for animals was the spark that
started this process.

And for my supportive husband, Ray,
who always encourages me
to reach for the stars.

Scarlett the Sloth was trying to sleep. Scarlett was an excellent sleeper. But not today.

Today someone was making a racket under her tree.

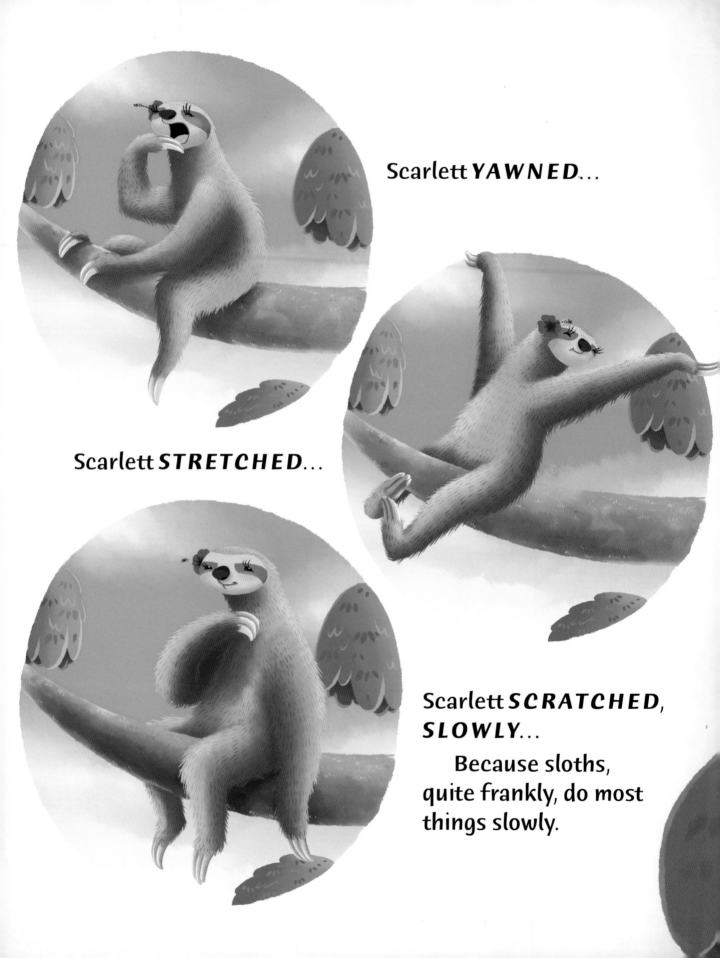

Scarlett **YAWNED**…

Scarlett **STRETCHED**…

Scarlett **SCRATCHED, SLOWLY**…
Because sloths, quite frankly, do most things slowly.

Then Scarlett headed down
to see who was making all
that noise.

Under the tree sat Bo Bo and Winston.

Bo Bo was crying. Very loudly. And Winston could not calm him.

"What's wrong, Bo Bo?" Scarlett asked.

"Mr. Cuddles is missing," he sobbed. "I can't sleep without him."

Bo Bo wailed **LOUDER**. And one thing was clear:
No one would sleep until Mr. Cuddles was found.
"I'll find him," Scarlett declared.

"You can't find Mr. Cuddles," said Jaguar Jax. "You are too slow."

"And too sleepy," added Dart Frog Daisy.

"Sloths are good at eating and snoozing and not much more," said Anaconda Andy.

"I can run faster than anyone," said Jaguar Jax. "I'll find Mr. Cuddles."

"I can hop higher than anyone," said Dart Frog Daisy. "I'll find Mr. Cuddles."

"I can slither longer than anyone," said Anaconda Andy. "I'll find Mr. Cuddles."

And with that they all took off.

Scarlett tried to take off too.

But sloths are not made for taking off.

Maybe they're right, Scarlett thought.
Maybe I'm not good for much at all.

But that wasn't true.

For one thing, Scarlett was **EXTREMELY** good at hanging around.

And that's what she did.

"Don't worry, Bo Bo," Scarlett said, swinging from a branch. "Let's think. Where did you see Mr. Cuddles last?"

It was hard to cry and think at the same time, so Bo Bo stopped crying.

"Up in my tree," Bo Bo said.

"It's all my fault," Winston frowned. "I told Bo Bo to come down for a banana, and when he went back up, Mr. Cuddles was gone."

Scarlett decided to search Bo Bo's branch.

Which took some time because sloths, as you know, are very slow.

Inch by slow inch, Scarlett climbed higher and higher. When she stopped to rest, she saw…

…Anaconda Andy and Dart Frog Daisy. Andy was taking a sunbath. He seemed to have forgotten all about Mr. Cuddles.

Dart Frog Daisy was hopping high. In fact, she was mostly leaping and not really looking.

Jaguar Jax raced through the trees. *He's so fast, he's sure to find Mr. Cuddles first*, Scarlett thought.

But that didn't stop Scarlett. She climbed higher and higher until she reached Bo Bo's branch. And there she found a long, blue feather. "A clue!" said Scarlett.

Inch by slow inch, Scarlett
headed down.
    So slowly, she had plenty of
time to think about her clue.

…and thought…

…and thought.

And by the time she reached Bo Bo, she had something important to say.

"Stand up, Winston."

"Mr. Cuddles fell out of the tree," Scarlett said. "And Winston sat on him."

Everyone in the forest heard the news, and Scarlett was very pleased with herself.

"Sloths are good at eating and sleeping—and *so* much more!" Scarlett announced.

Then inch by slow inch, she headed up the tree, closed her eyes, and fell fast asleep.

Glossary of Jungle Animals

Capuchin Monkey – Bo Bo

- **Scientific Name**: *Cebinae*
- **Classification**: Mammal
- **Habitat**: Tropical rainforests, dry forests, and mangrove forests
- **Life Span**: 40 to 45 years
- **Diet**: Omnivore
- **Range**: Central and South America
- **Status**: Population Stable

Capuchin monkeys, commonly found in the tropical rainforests of Central and South America, are primates that are considered among the most intelligent of the New World monkeys. They are named for their "caps" of hair, which resemble the cowls of Capuchin monks. These monkeys are round-headed with a stocky build, prehensile tails, and opposable thumbs. Their body is 12 to 22 inches long, with a tail about the same length. Fur colors range from pale to dark brown or black, with white facial markings in some of the four species.

Fun Facts
- Capuchins live together in groups of six to forty members.
- The young Capuchin monkeys cling to their mother's chest. When they have matured somewhat, they move to her back.
- Apart from a midday nap, the Capuchin monkey spends its entire day searching for food and hanging out in trees.

Capybara – Winston

- **Scientific Name**: *Hydrochoerus hydrochaeris*
- **Classification**: Mammal
- **Habitat**: Swampy, grassy regions bordering rivers, ponds, streams, and lakes
- **Life Span**: 10 years
- **Diet**: Herbivore
- **Range**: Central and South America
- **Status**: Population Stable

A capybara is the largest rodent in the world! Standing 2 feet tall at its shoulder and built somewhat like a barrel with legs, the "capy" has long, light brown, shaggy hair, a face that looks like a beaver's, no tail, and slightly webbed feet. Originally thought to be a pig of some sort, we now know that the capybara is a rodent, closely related to cavies and guinea pigs.

Fun Facts
- A fully grown capybara reaches 4 feet in length and weighs 140 pounds. Females are larger than males.
- Capybaras will live next to water, preferably next to a muddy river where it will find plenty of aquatic plants to eat. Besides getting nutrients from water, they will also use it to protect themselves from predators. They will use dry places to rest.
- Capybaras can stay underwater for five minutes in order to hide themselves.

Dart Frog - Daisy

- **Scientific Name**: *Dendrobates tinctorius*
- **Classification**: Amphibian
- **Habitat**: Tropical rainforests
- **Life Span**: 3 to 15 years
- **Diet**: Carnivore
- **Range**: Central and South America
- **Status**: Critically Endangered

These frogs are considered one of Earth's most toxic, or poisonous, species. With a range of bright colors—yellows, oranges, reds, greens, blues—they aren't just big show-offs either. Those colorful designs tell potential predators, "I'm toxic. Don't eat me." Scientists think that poison dart frogs get their toxicity from some of the insects they eat. How do poison dart frogs capture their prey? Slurp! with a long, sticky tongue that darts out and zaps the unsuspecting bug! The frogs eat many kinds of small insects, including fruit flies, ants, termites, young crickets, and tiny beetles, which are the ones scientists think may be responsible for the frogs' toxicity. Poison dart frogs live in the rainforests of Central and South America.

Fun Facts

- Poison dart frogs are one of the most brightly colored creatures on earth.
- Some poison dart frogs show unusual habits in that they're often seen to carry both eggs and tadpoles on their back.
- A group of poison frogs is called an "army."

Giant Anteater

- **Scientific Name**: *Myrmecophaga tridactyla*
- **Classification**: Mammal
- **Habitat**: Forests
- **Life Span**: 14 years
- **Diet**: Carnivore
- **Range**: Central and South America
- **Status**: Vulnerable

Anteaters have no teeth, but their long tongues can lap up to 35,000 ants and termites each day. The giant anteater can reach 7 feet long from the tip of its snout to the end of its tail. The anteater uses its sharp claws to tear an opening into an anthill and put its long snout and tongue to work, but it must eat quickly, flicking its tongue up to 160 times per minute. Ants fight back with painful stings, so an anteater may spend only a minute feasting on each mound. Anteaters never destroy a nest, preferring to return and feed again in the future. Anteaters are generally solitary animals. Females have a single offspring once a year, which can sometimes be seen riding on its mother's back.

Fun Facts

- The giant anteater's tongue is typically two feet long—24 inches! No other mammal has a tongue as long relative to its body size.
- Giant anteaters have the lowest body temperature of any mammal. Because bugs don't provide anteaters with a ton of energy, they have slow metabolisms and a body temperature of only 90.86 degrees Fahrenheit.
- The giant anteater has poor eyesight, but its sense of smell is 40 times more sensitive than that of humans.

Golden Lion Tamarin - Finn, Quinn, and Brynn

- **Scientific Name**: *Leontopithecus rosalia*
- **Classification**: Mammal
- **Habitat**: Forests
- **Life Span**: 15 years
- **Diet**: Omnivore
- **Range**: Central and South America
- **Status**: Endangered

Lion tamarins take their name from their impressive manes—thick rings of hair reminiscent of Africa's great cat—the lion. The golden lion tamarin forms social family groups. Males help raise their offspring, and often carry their young on their backs in between feedings. Tamarin young are often twins and sometimes triplets. Golden lion tamarins live primarily in the trees. They sleep in hollowed out trees at night and forage by day while traveling from branch to branch. Long fingers help them stay aloft and snare insects, fruit, lizards, and birds.

Fun Facts

- Golden lion tamarins are usually monogamous.
- There are only about 1,500 golden lion tamarins left in the wild. Another 500 live in zoos around the world.
- Females usually give birth to twins. All the members of her group will help her to take care of the babies, but the dad helps the most.

Green Anaconda - Andy

- **Scientific Name**: *Eunectes murinus*
- **Classification**: Reptile
- **Habitat**: Freshwater forests
- **Life Span**: 10 years
- **Diet**: Carnivore
- **Range**: South America and Florida
- **Status**: Population Stable

The green anaconda is the largest snake in the world when both weight and length are considered. It can reach a length of 30 feet and weigh up to 550 pounds. The green anaconda is a member of a family of snakes called constrictors. Constrictors are not venomous snakes. They don't kill prey by delivering venom through a bite. Instead, constrictors wrap their bodies around their prey and squeeze until it stops breathing. The giant snake opens its mouth wide enough to swallow its victim—sometimes fish or caiman (relatives of crocodiles) and even jaguars and small deer. Anaconda jaws are held together with stretchy ligaments, so they can open wide enough to swallow prey whole.

Fun Facts

- Green anacondas reproduce by "ovoviviparity," which means that these reptiles' offspring emerge from eggs before leaving their mothers' bodies. When the big day finally arrives, they wriggle out as fully formed youngsters. A healthy anaconda mom can squeeze out over 30 babies per litter.
- Anacondas can remain underwater for up to ten minutes at a time.
- Anacondas have four rows of teeth on their upper jaws.

Jaguar - Jax

- **Scientific Name**: *Panthera onca*
- **Classification**: Mammal
- **Habitat**: Swampy savannas and tropical rainforests
- **Life Span**: 12 to 15 years
- **Diet**: Carnivore
- **Range**: Central and South America
- **Status**: Near Threatened

Jaguars are the largest of South America's big cats. Today significant numbers of jaguars are found only in remote regions of South and Central America—particularly in the Amazon Basin. Unlike many other cats, jaguars do not avoid water; in fact, they are quite good swimmers. Rivers provide prey in the form of fish, turtles, or caimans—small, alligatorlike animals. Jaguars also eat larger animals such as deer, peccaries, capybaras, and tapirs. They sometimes climb trees to prepare an ambush, killing their prey with one powerful bite.

Fun Facts
- The jaguar is the third-largest of the big cats after the tiger and the lion, and it is the largest of all the big cats in the Americas.
- Jaguars roam, hunt, and live alone, only coming together to mate.
- The jaguar has a very powerful jaw. Its bite exerts more force than that of a lion.

Ocelot

- **Scientific Name**: *Leopardus pardalis*
- **Classification**: Mammal
- **Habitat**: Tropical forests, as well as mangrove forests, coastal marshes, thorn scrub, and savanna grasslands
- **Life Span**: 10 to 13 years
- **Diet**: Carnivore
- **Range**: Southwestern United States, Mexico, Central America, and South America
- **Status**: Population Stable

Twice the size of the average house cat, the ocelot is a sleek animal with a gorgeous dappled coat. These largely nocturnal cats use keen sight and hearing to hunt rabbits, rodents, iguanas, fish, and frogs. They also take to the trees and stalk monkeys or birds. Unlike many cats, they do not avoid water and can swim well. Like other cats, ocelots are adapted for eating meat.

Fun Facts
- The ocelot is also known as the dwarf leopard.
- The ocelot's primary habitat requirement is dense vegetative cover. Ocelots are found in open areas only when it's cloudy or at night when there is a new moon.
- Ocelots are very active, traveling from 1 to 4 miles per night. Males travel nearly twice as far as females.

Scarlet Macaw – Maggie

- **Scientific Name**: *Ara macao*
- **Classification**: Bird
- **Habitat**: Tropical forests
- **Life Span**: 40 to 50 years
- **Diet**: Omnivore
- **Range**: Central and South America
- **Status**: Population Stable

Macaws are king-sized members of the parrot family and have typical parrot features. Their large, strong, curved beaks are designed to crush nuts and seeds. Their strong, agile toes are used like hands to grasp things. Loud screeching and squawking voices help make their presence known in dense rainforests. They are also famous for their bright colors, which seem bold and conspicuous to us but really blend in well with the green leaves, red and yellow fruits, and bluish shadows of their forest homes.

Fun Facts

- Scarlet macaws are one of the most intelligent bird species. It has been said that they can have the intelligence of a four- to eight-year-old child with the emotional intelligence of a two-year-old.
- The scarlet macaw generally mates for life. The female usually lays 1 to 4 eggs and both males and females care for the young.
- Their intelligence and beauty are two reasons why people keep them as pets, but because of their ability to become aggressive they do not make good pets for kids.

Sloth – Scarlett

- **Scientific Name**: *Bradypus variegatus*
- **Classification**: Mammal
- **Habitat**: Forests
- **Life Span**: 3 to 15 years
- **Diet**: Herbivore
- **Range**: Central and South America
- **Status**: Population Stable

These slow tree-dwellers sleep up to 20 hours a day! And even when they are awake, they barely move at all. They are so inactive that algae will grow on their fur. Sloths live in the tropical forests of Central and South America. With their long arms and shaggy fur, they resemble monkeys, but they are more closely related to armadillos and anteaters. They can be 2 to 2 ½ feet long and, depending on species, weigh from 8 to 17 pounds. There are two main species of sloths identified by whether they have two or three claws on their front feet. The two species are quite similar in appearance, with roundish heads, sad-looking eyes, tiny ears, and stubby tails. Two-toed sloths are slightly bigger and tend to spend more time hanging upside-down than their three-toed cousins, which will often sit upright in the fork of a tree branch. Three-toed sloths have facial coloring that makes them look like they're always smiling. They also have two extra neck vertebrae that allow them to turn their heads almost all the way around!

Fun Facts

- Sloths have a four-part stomach that very slowly digests the tough leaves they eat. It can sometimes take up to a month for them to digest a meal.
- The slow movements and unique thick fur of the sloth make it a great habitat for other creatures such as moths, beetles, cockroaches, and fungi.
- Sloths can extend their tongues 10 to 12 inches out of their mouths